Attn: Thomas E. Crice, Esq.
One Boston Place, Suite 2600
Boston, MA 02108

Printed and bound in the United States of America

ISBN 978-0-9996853-0-3 (hardcover)
Library of Congress Control Number 2017962280

Book design by Clare Letendre

The illustrations in this book were created using colored pencil and acrylic on paper.

Birds of a Feather

A Children's Story of Love, Loss, and What Came Next

By **Tom Crice**
Illustrated by Ellen Rakatansky

For Emma and Jacob

Chapter 1

When I was little, my grandfather was my very best friend. His real name was LeRoy but I called him Pop.

He had a big, soft belly and lived in a small Texas town.

It had one grocery store and one café. People grew a lot of cotton there.

My mom and I lived in a big city. It had a subway, tons of places to eat, and lots and lots of people.

Mama grew a patch of flowers in our tiny front yard.

Pop had a whole shop full of flowers.

We visited him a lot. Sometimes we stayed all summer.

Those days were hot!

Pop's shop had a cooler big enough to walk around in.

He kept so many flowers in there the air was foggy with color and sweet smells.

In the back was a wooden case of icy cold soda in glass bottles. Every day at three o'clock he took one out and we drank it together.

My job was to help load his delivery truck.

Then we rode around all morning giving people flowers.

Pop drove.

I picked the radio stations.

After work, we'd go to the café for lunch.

As soon as we reached our table the lady would bring us warm rolls and butter in a red basket.

We'd race eating them all and she would laugh.

"Y'all sure are birds of a feather," she'd say in her slow drawl.

In Texas that meant Pop and I were a lot alike.

Then she'd bring another basket, this time piled really high.

Afterward, full of rolls and soda, Pop and I took naps together under a ceiling fan. It felt good to lie on Pop's big belly.

I remember days and days like that. Evenings, we played dominos and croquet and caught fireflies in the backyard.

Of all the people I knew, Pop was the only one who was always glad to see me, who liked me for the boy I was.

I really loved him.

Then one day, when we were back at our city home, Mama told me he was gone. My granddad had died.

Mama took me with her to Texas, so we could tell him goodbye, she said.

But when we arrived, there wasn't anyone to say goodbye to.

The flower shop was closed. The cooler was empty and hot. It looked gray inside. The delivery truck was gone.

I asked to see the lady who brought the rolls but Mama said, "No." Instead she took me to Pop's church.

When we got there it was full of people. Up front was a long wooden box on a stand.

There were flowers all around it. They looked and smelled just like the ones Pop and I used to deliver.

"Now it's time to say goodbye," Mama told me.

But when I looked inside the box it wasn't Pop in there.

I knew it wasn't him because he didn't smile at me once, even though I looked and looked and waited and waited.

I didn't want to lie on his big stomach.

At home we used to have an old television and I watched lots of shows on it. That was fun until one day it stopped working.

Then it wasn't a television anymore. It was just a broken thing full of stuff that didn't work.

Inside the long box with all the flowers around it was kind of like that.

An old woman smiled, put her hand on my shoulder, and told me she had known Pop ever since he was my size.

She said, "You should be happy because he's in heaven now."

I wasn't.

Mama cried and cried. The people all sang.

Chapter 2

Back at home the days passed into weeks. I went to school like always. I played with other kids like always.

Sometimes Mama and I rode the subway train downtown to eat doughnuts and see movies.

It was all fun.

But not as fun as it used to be.

I kept thinking about Pop and the long wooden box.

But I didn't tell anyone I did that, not my teacher or my friends and especially not Mama.

She was still sad too.

I didn't want Mama to know I wasn't glad Pop was in heaven, or that I hadn't ever said goodbye.

I didn't want to hurt her with my feelings.

Some days I wasn't sad at all. I was angry. Pop had gone away without me and he hadn't even said why or goodbye.

Once I was so mad I stomped all over my mother's pretty fall flowers until they were flat and dirty.

Later, when she asked me what happened to them, I said I didn't know.

Then I felt even worse.

Chapter 3

One day, after fall was gone and winter was nearly over, Mama and I headed downtown on the subway train.

The train made lots of stops to let people on and off. At the fourth stop, just as the doors slid open, two little birds flew right in!

They swooped back and forth from one end of the train car to the other, cheeping and flapping.

Everyone ducked and laughed as they whizzed by.

The doors closed and the train took off, little birds and all.

They found a perch on the upper handrail. It was slippery but they hung on.

They kept touching beaks and wings and snuggling together. They were mates and they were frightened a little bit.

All of a sudden they were moving fast but they weren't flying. There was lots of light but no sun at all.

They didn't understand anything about trains or being underground. They only knew about trees and sky.

13

At the next station the train jerked to a stop and one of the birds slipped off their perch. He squawked in surprise and flapped his wings a lot.

The train doors opened and he flapped and flopped right out onto the platform!

He got to his feet, shook himself, and called out to his mate. She answered and flew back and forth in the train car.

But she didn't understand what was happening. The doors closed and off we went, her still inside and him left behind.

She landed on the empty seat across from me. We looked and looked at each other.

I could see her heart beating in her chest.

She was as alone as I felt.

I was scared like her.

Chapter 4

As the train rolled along, a man opened his lunch bag and tore some of his sandwich into little pieces.

He tossed one bit onto the seat next to the little bird and she gobbled it up.

The train slowed as it entered the next station.

The man threw another piece onto the floor in front of the doors.

The bird flew down and ate that one too.

The train stopped, the doors opened, and the man threw more pieces outside, onto the platform.

The little bird went after them, hopping right through the doors.

She swallowed one and looked all around, up and down and right and left. Things were different.

"Cheep!" she said.

As the doors closed she looked right at me. "Cheep, cheep!"

The last I saw of her she took off flying, heading somewhere I couldn't imagine.

I wondered whether she would find her mate again.

Would she ever get back outside, back to trees and wind and sun?

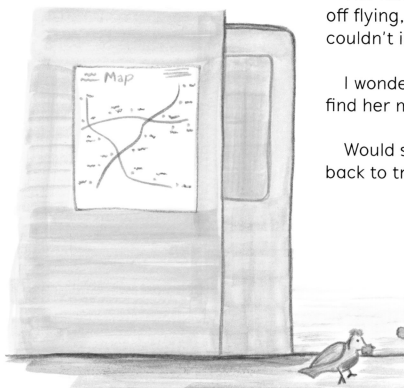

Maybe she'd say to herself, "My mate is in heaven."

Maybe she'd say "Goodbye" to him.

But I didn't think so. She was a bird, not a person.

Then again, I was a person and I didn't say those things either, about my Pop. So we were kind of the same.

"That little bird can fly," I thought. "It must be really exciting."

I imagined her zipping through the subway, eating yummy food.

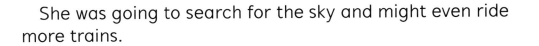

She was going to search for the sky and might even ride more trains.

Even if she missed her mate, life was still a big adventure.

I looked at Mama and smiled.

"Cheep, cheep," I said and tucked my hands under my arms, flapping my elbows like wings.

"I'm a bird!"

I laughed so hard and couldn't stop. I fell over and Mama said I was too-oo-oo silly.

But she was laughing too.

Chapter 5

That afternoon Mama and I went to a restaurant on top of the tallest building in the whole city.

We ate cheesecake, sitting way up in the sky at eye level with clouds, while men played violins.

Birds flew right by us.

After, in the park, we saw a little girl walking six dogs as big as ponies on long leashes. It looked like they were walking her!

Nearby, a man on a street corner blew real fire right out of his mouth. People clapped and gave him coins.

On the way back to the subway station we stopped at a store full of gardening things.

Mama said we needed new flowers to plant in our front yard patch.

I chose lots of different colored ones and paid for them all myself.

I had been saving my allowance money.

"I'd like to plant them," I said, "when the weather is a little warmer."

Mama nodded and gave me a big, long hug.

I think maybe she knew what I had done to our other front yard flowers.

"They'll be very pretty," she said. "Pop would have liked them."

I pictured that, the three of us together, looking at the flowers in bloom on a hot summer day.

In my mind the light around us was soft and rosy, like it had been in the cooler.

I was glad I hadn't said goodbye to Pop because now it felt just like he was there with me, even if he wasn't really.

I was so happy that day.

I ran everywhere, flapping my arm-wings and cheeping, looking at everything and wondering and marveling.

The world was just chock-full of amazing stuff.

And it's still just as amazing, all these years and years later. Now there's even a kid who calls me Pop.

Imagine that.

Things are so different from how they used to be. But they're also kind of the same.

I'm sure glad I never stopped flapping my arm-wings.

"Cheep, cheep!"

THE END

As a boy, **Tom** spent a fair amount of time in Texas, delivering flowers and eating rolls with his grandfather. He grew up to be a lawyer, raised a terrific kid of his own, and traveled the world whenever he could. He lives in Cambridge, MA, where he works, writes, and occasionally takes a math class.

Ellen lives in Cambridge, MA, where she works as a business analyst, musician, and artist.